Hello, Family Members,

Learning to read is one of the most important accomplishments of early childhood. **Hello Reader!** books are designed to help children become skilled readers who like to read. Beginning readers learn to read by remembering frequently used words like "the," "is," and "and"; by using phonics skills to decode new words; and by interpreting picture and text clues. These books provide both the stories children enjoy and the structure they need to read fluently and independently. Here are suggestions for helping your child *before*, *during*, and *after* reading:

Before
- Look at the cover and pictures and have your child predict what the story is about.
- Read the story to your child.
- Encourage your child to chime in with familiar words and phrases.
- Echo read with your child by reading a line first and having your child read it after you do.

During
- Have your child think about a word he or she does not recognize right away. Provide hints such as "Let's see if we know the sounds" and "Have we read other words like this one?"
- Encourage your child to use phonics skills to sound out new words.
- Provide the word for your child when more assistance is needed so that he or she does not struggle and the experience of reading with you is a positive one.
- Encourage your child to have fun by reading with a lot of expression . . . like an actor!

After
- Have your child keep lists of interesting and favorite words.
- Encourage your child to read the books over and over again. Have him or her read to brothers, sisters, grandparents, and even teddy bears. Repeated readings develop confidence in young readers.
- Talk about the stories. Ask and answer questions. Share ideas about the funniest and most interesting characters and events in the stories.

I do hope that you and your child enjoy this book.

—Francie Alexander
Reading Specialist,
Scholastic's Learning V̶

For all the great students and teachers at Mary McDowell
Center for Learning in Brooklyn, New York
— K.M.

To the skeletons
in the closet
— M.S.

ISBN 0-439-31941-2

Text copyright © 2001 by Kate McMullan.
Illustrations copyright © 2001 by Mavis Smith.
All rights reserved. Published by Scholastic Inc.
SCHOLASTIC, HELLO READER, CARTWHEEL BOOKS,
and associated logos are trademarks and/or
registered trademarks of Scholastic Inc.

Library of Congress Cataloging-in-Publication Data

McMullan, Kate.
    Fluffy's trick-or-treat / by Kate McMullan ; illustrated by Mavis Smith.
       p. cm. — (Hello reader! Level 3)
    "Cartwheel books."
    Summary: When Fluffy the guinea pig goes to Emma's house over
Halloween weekend, he goes trick-or-treating dressed as a circus performer
and does some very fancy tricks.
      ISBN 0-439-31941-2 (pbk.)
        [1. Guinea pigs—Fiction. 2. Halloween—Fiction.] I. Smith, Mavis,
        ill. II. Title. III. Series.
PZT.M2295 Fk 2001
[E]—dc21   2001032255

10 9 8 7 6 5 4 3 2   04 05

Printed in the U.S.A.   23
First printing, October 2001

FLUFFY'S TRICK·OR·TREAT

by Kate McMullan

Illustrated by Mavis Smith

Hello Reader! — Level 3

SCHOLASTIC INC.

Cartwheel B·O·O·K·S®

New York Toronto London Auckland Sydney
Mexico City New Delhi Hong Kong

Fluffy's Trick

"Saturday is Halloween," said Ms. Day.
"Who would like to take Fluffy
home for Halloween weekend?"
"Me! Me! Me!" all the kids called out.
When you're hot, you're hot,
thought Fluffy.
And I am one hot pig.

"How about you, Emma?" said Ms. Day.

"All right!" said Emma.

Lucky you, thought Fluffy.

On Saturday afternoon, Jasmine
came over to Emma's house.
The girls made fancy treat bags.
"This is your treat bag, Fluffy,"
said Emma.
Treat? thought Fluffy.
Did somebody say treat?

"Let's put on our costumes!"
said Emma.
She put on a clown outfit.
Jasmine dressed up
as a tightrope walker.
"We have a circus costume
for you, too, Fluffy," said Emma.
Huh? thought Fluffy.

Emma picked up one of her dolls.

She took off the doll's swimsuit.

Jasmine held it up.

"I think this will fit him," she said.

Him who? thought Fluffy.

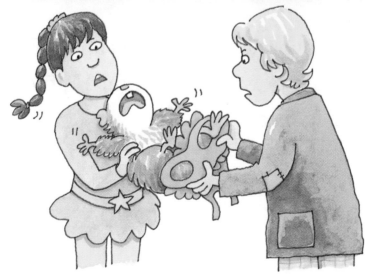

Jasmine picked up Fluffy.

Emma tried to put Fluffy's feet
through the leg holes of the swimsuit.

Fluffy kicked like crazy.

"Oh, stop it, Fluffy," said Emma.

"There! All dressed!"

It doesn't get any worse than this,
thought Fluffy.

Jasmine put the doll's swim cap on Fluffy.
Okay, this is worse, thought Fluffy.
MUCH worse.

Emma picked up a stuffed horse.

She put Fluffy on its back.

"Fluffy the bareback rider!" said Emma.

Bear? thought Fluffy.

Did somebody say BEAR?

"Stand up on the horse's back,"
Emma told Fluffy.

Why would I want to do that?
thought Fluffy.

"Come on, Fluffy," said Jasmine.

"Do your trick!"

Anything to get this over with,
thought Fluffy.

Fluffy slowly stood up.

"Ride 'em, Fluffy!" said Jasmine.

"What a great trick!" said Emma.

Right, thought bareback-rider Fluffy.

Now where's my treat?

Fluffy Rides Again

Emma put on clown makeup.

Jasmine put on tightrope-walker makeup.

"Your turn, Fluffy," said Emma.

Uh-uh, thought Fluffy. **Not this pig!**

"Fluffy doesn't need makeup,"
said Jasmine.
Phew! thought Fluffy.
Emma picked up the treat bags.
She said, "Let's go trick-or-treating!"
Go OUT? thought Fluffy. **Like THIS?**

Just then Emma's dog, Skippy,
came into the room.

"Hey, let's dress Skippy up!" said Jasmine.

"He can come trick-or-treating with us."

Emma put a T-shirt on Skippy.

Jasmine tied a scarf around his neck.

"Skippy the circus dog!" said Emma.

Skippy didn't seem to mind.

He wagged his tail.

Skippy looks silly, thought Fluffy.

But I look sillier.

The girls walked to the house
next door. Emma rang the bell.
A mom with a little boy opened the door.
"Trick-or-treat!" said Emma and Jasmine.
"Hello, circus girls!" said the mom.
"Can your circus dog do a trick?"
"Sure," said Emma. "Watch."

"Sit up, circus dog!" said Emma.

Skippy sat up.

"Shake hands, circus dog!" said Emma.

Skippy held out a paw.

"Go to sleep, circus dog!" said Emma.

Skippy lay down.

He put his paws over his eyes.

"Nice doggie!" said the little boy.

"Fluffy can do a trick, too," said Emma.

Now you're talking, thought Fluffy.

Emma put Fluffy onto the stuffed horse.

Fluffy stood up.

Tah-dah! he thought.

"Nice mousie!" said the little boy.

Mousie? thought Fluffy.

He can't mean ME!

"Treat time!" said the mom.

The girls opened their treat bags.

They opened Fluffy's treat bag, too.

The little boy put candy into the bags.

Can we go home now? thought Fluffy.

The girls went to the next house.

Jasmine rang the bell.

A dad with two little girls
opened the door.

Emma and Jasmine said, "Trick-or-treat!"

"We can show you circus tricks," Emma said.

Skippy did his tricks.

The dad and the little girls clapped.

Then it was Fluffy's turn.

Watch this! thought Fluffy.

He stood on the stuffed horse's back.

He bent over and spread his arms.

He raised one leg out behind him.

He pointed his toes.

Tah-dah! thought Fluffy.

"That's not so hard," said one little girl.

The girls gave out treats.

Fluffy's treat bag was filling up.

But Fluffy didn't care.

No one liked his trick!

At every house, Skippy did his tricks.

Everyone clapped and cheered.

But no one clapped for Fluffy.

I will show them! thought Fluffy.

I will be a REAL bareback rider.

At the next house, Emma put Fluffy
onto the stuffed horse.
But Fluffy jumped onto Skippy's back.
"Fluffy!" cried Emma.
Skippy just wagged his tail.
Tah-dah! thought Fluffy.

Just then, Skippy saw a squirrel.
He ran into the backyard after it.
Fluffy bounced up and down
on Skippy's back.
He rolled over and over.
Fluffy grabbed Skippy's tail.
He held on tight.
Yikes! thought bareback-rider Fluffy.

Skippy ran to a tree. He jumped up.
He barked at the squirrel.
Bareback-rider Fluffy bounced
some more. But he held on tight.

Emma and Jasmine ran to Skippy.

Emma grabbed his collar.

She got him to settle down.

Jasmine picked up Fluffy.

"Fluffy!" she said. "Are you all right?"

Sure, thought bareback-rider Fluffy.

Just don't ask to see THAT trick again.

Fluffy's Treat Bag

"I have to take Skippy home," Emma said.
"Let's go," said Jasmine. "Our treat bags
are full anyway. Fluffy's treat bag is *really* full."
It is? thought Fluffy. **Oh, boy!**

The circus girls started for home.
They saw two pirates walking
toward them. One pirate was Wade.
The other was Jared from Mr. Lee's class.
He had a parrot on his shoulder.

Jasmine took a closer look.
The parrot was Kiss!
"Fluffy!" said Jasmine. "Look who's here!"
She held bareback-rider Fluffy
up to parrot Kiss.

The two pigs looked at each other.
**I promise not to tell anyone
how silly you look,** said Fluffy,
**if you promise not to tell anyone
how silly I look.**
Deal, said Kiss.

The girls went back to Emma's house.
They took off Fluffy's swim cap.
Ahhh! thought Fluffy. **That's better!**
The girls emptied out the treat bags
onto the kitchen counter.
"Don't eat too many treats, girls,"
said Emma's mom.
"Save room for some of my soup!"

"Here are your treats, Fluffy," said Emma.

Fluffy ran over to his treats.

He sniffed at them.

They smelled funny.

These are not good treats for a pig!

thought Fluffy.

Fluffy sniffed the air.

He smelled something good to eat.

He scurried off to find it.

The girls were busy sorting
their treats.

They did not see him go.

Fluffy sniffed at a grocery bag.
He poked his head in.
Aha! thought Fluffy.
He crawled inside.

Emma's mom put an onion
into the soup pot. She reached
into the bag for the carrots.
"*Aaaaaah!*" she cried.
Emma and Jasmine ran over to her.
They looked into the grocery bag.

Hi, there, thought Fluffy.
He bit into a carrot.

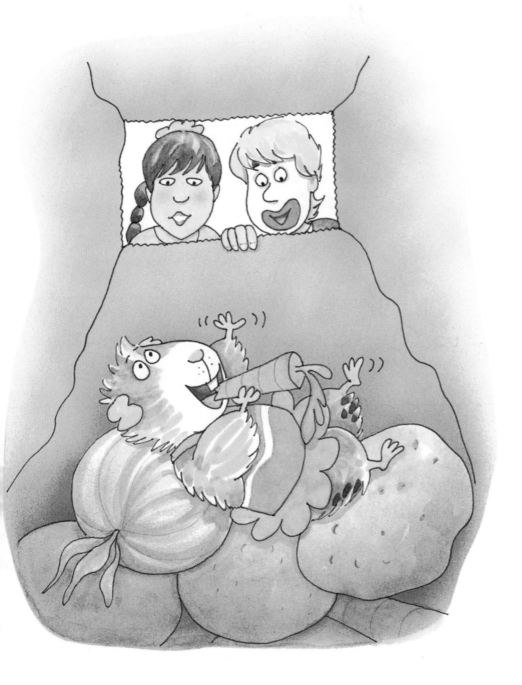

Now THIS is what I call a treat bag,
thought Fluffy.
Happy Halloween!